WALTZING IN TRIOLET

A SNAPSHOT OF CREATION

PHIL LOWE

ISBN: 978-1-63649-237-7   (Paperback Edition)
ISBN: 978-1-63649-238-4   (Hardcover Edition)
ISBN: 978-1-63649-236-0   (E-book Edition)

Some characters and events in this book are fictitious. Any similarity to real persons, living or dead, is coincidental and not intended by the author.

Book Ordering Information

Phone Number: 315 288-7939 ext. 1000 or 347-901-4920
Email: info@globalsummithouse.com
Global Summit House
www.globalsummithouse.com

Printed in the United States of America

Much love and gratitude to my wife Betty and our two daughters Kim and Susan for their endless love and patience that gave me freedom and time to wander through the world of nature with my camera.

Endless Love

Love

a never ending quest
a journey without scale.

No ruler measures
widening breadth
nor gauge controls
its fathom's depth.

And to the heights
that it ascends
no canopy contains,

for in its seeking
soul will find
an endless
source remains.

Introduction to Triolet

The Triolet has two rhyme sounds,
lines two and eight repeat.

Lines one-four-seven complete the round,
the Triolet has two rhyme sounds.

In this French style the poet is bound,
no room for lines that cheat.

The Triolet has two rhyme sounds,
lines two and eight repeat.

The Triolet is an Old World French, Fixed Form Poem that dates back to the13th century. The poem consists of eight lines, has two rhyme sounds and is heavy on refrains. The Triolet is part of the Rondeau family of poems, which in turn is derived from "dance-rounds," with singing. The refrain was sung by the chorus and the variable sections by the leader. The word "Triolet" has two pronunciations in English according to several dictionaries. The first rhymes with "let" and the second rhymes with "Chevrolet."

The Triolet is as out of style as bow-ties and high-heels at a baseball game. However, I find style to be no more than conformity to solicit approval and praise from peers. My choice for this book is to avoid conformity and use the form most suited to my purpose.

State of Balance

Spring equinox is a balanced state,
where day and night share equal time.
The appointed moment is never late,
Spring equinox is a balanced state.
No government body can legislate
a law to disrupt the prime.
Spring equinox is a balanced state,
where night and day share equal time.

Pink Dogwood

Springtime Magic

In springtime life is renewable,
gives us space to rewrite lines.
Editing past deeds is doable,
in springtime life is renewable.
Our work is always reviewable,
subject to change in design.
In springtime life is renewable,
gives us space to rewrite lines.

*Cardinal
Flower*

When Spring Comes

I will sit beneath a weeping willow
on the bank of a flowing stream.

While lichens cling to rocky pillows,
I will sit beneath a weeping willow.

Water music playing soft and mellow
will add new magic to my dream.

I will sit beneath a weeping willow,
on the bank of a flowing stream.

Creator's Quills

True words of wisdom come to light,
as feathered pen of spirit moves.
Sealed with breath of clear insight
true words of wisdom come to light.
Mind's illusions soon take flight,
myth and fable sustain reproves.
True words of wisdom come to light,
as feathered pen of spirit moves.

Cattle Egret

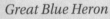

Great Blue Heron

Constant Measure

Love, the crowning jewel of soul
reflects in constant measure.
Adore for life removes blindfold,
love, the crowning jewel of soul.
Charity imbeds like ink on scroll,
life's storybook of treasures.
Love, the crowning jewel of soul,
reflects in constant measure.

Work

Work, the tuning fork of soul,
brings focus to endeavor.

Self-awareness,
life's true goal,
work, the tuning fork of soul.

Idle hands on blind patrol
not meant to last forever.

Work, the tuning fork of soul,
brings focus to endeavor.

Buying and Selling

When we buy and when we sell
the scales should be in balance.

Toiling hands should fill their pail,
when we buy and when we sell.

Those with songs and words to tell
should suffer no imbalance.

When we buy and when we sell
the scales should be in balance.

Unto Its Self

The essence of love has no boundary,
no divide to pull it apart.
Sufficient to itself in its foundry,
the essence of love has no boundary.
Romantics should approach with due chary,
true love has no stop and no start.
The essence of love has no boundary,
no divide to pull it apart.

Bright Light of Love

Bright light of love falls soft on all,
no shadows cast on race or creed.
No trite religious forces stall,
bright light of love falls soft on all.
Dark side of man can build a wall,
for all who sponsor war and greed.
Bright light of love falls soft on all,
no shadows cast on race or creed.

Cause and Effect

Action and reaction brings
opportunity,
a chance to make things better.
Motion never receives immunity,
action and reaction brings
opportunity.
Balance is the art of serenity,
freedom to act and not be a debtor.
Action and reaction brings
opportunity,
a chance to make things better.

A Work in Process

Human evolution a process,
evolving egos kill and maim.
Animal traits hint of regress,
human evolution a process.
Circle of time shows no
progress,
greed's motive is always
the same.
Human evolution a process,
evolving egos kill and maim.

Crime and Punishment

Like cloth we are woven together,
the loom yields diversified strings.
Crime and punishment we cannot sever,
like cloth we are woven together.
We've been taught this lesson forever,
how loud the school bell rings.
Like cloth we are woven together,
the loom yields diversified strings.

The Loom

Dark Night of Soul

In the cold of winter's night,
summer solstice lies at rest.
Sun-filled dreams a distant sight
in the cold of winter's night.
Vivid visions come to light,
bringing strength to face the test.
In the cold of winter's night,
summer solstice lies at rest.

Why Clouds

To grasp the beauty of sunrise,
understand the purpose of clouds.

Essence of light must be realized
to grasp the beauty of sunrise.

Each sunray in cryptic disguise
holds rainbows diffused by a shroud.

To grasp the beauty of sunrise,
understand the purpose of clouds.

Fire of Love

Eternal love's slow burning fire
turns ego into ashes.
Devours the sting of lust's desire,
eternal love's slow burning fire.
Release of fear,
does love require,
greed and anger crashes.
Eternal love's slow burning fire
turns ego into ashes.

Northern Cardinal

Door Key

Truth pounds doors of the mind,
hoping locked latches will lift.
Resistance crumbles in time,
truth pounds doors of the mind.
Awareness key to design,
balances wafting and drift.
Truth pounds doors of the mind,
hoping locked latches will lift.

Red Bellied Woodpecker

Self Awareness

As consciousness of self unfolds
new wisdom comes to light.
Astounding mysteries are told,
as consciousness of self unfolds.
Ego surrenders mind's blindfolds,
reveals soul's copyright.
As consciousness of self unfolds,
new wisdom comes to light.

Tufted Puffin

Idle Talk

Idle talk in search of self
breeds lonely moments deep within.
A cage of words leaves spirit deaf,
idle talk in search of self.
Ghosts of yesterday line the shelf,
the quest of soul to find a friend.
Idle talk in search of self,
leaves lonely moments deep within.

Horned Puffin

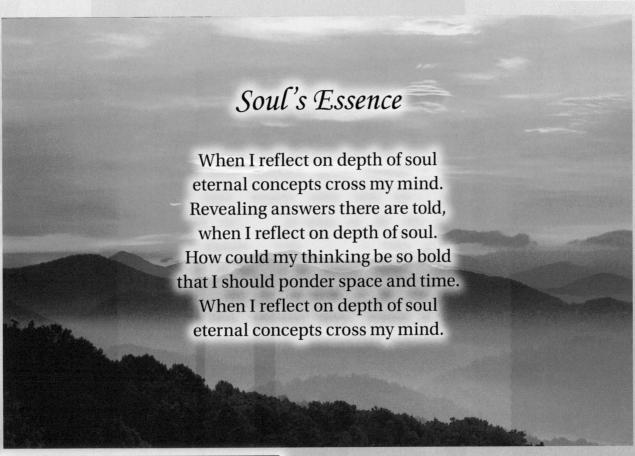

Soul's Essence

When I reflect on depth of soul
eternal concepts cross my mind.
Revealing answers there are told,
when I reflect on depth of soul.
How could my thinking be so bold
that I should ponder space and time.
When I reflect on depth of soul
eternal concepts cross my mind.

Icon of Soul

Beauty, an icon of soul's perception,
portraits locked in channels of the mind.
Guides our action by auto reflection,
beauty, an icon of soul's perception.
Mosaic inlays envision perfection,
holistic awareness, persona defined.
Beauty, an icon of soul's perception,
portraits locked in channels of the mind.

Giant Swallowtail Butterfly

Little Yellow Butterfly

Yellow Butterfly

Fluttering flower to flower,
sipping nectar from each floret.

Nectar gives soft wings power,
fluttering flower to flower.

Soul sees no need to cower,
wings strum in rhythmic duet.

Fluttering flower to flower,
sipping nectar from each floret.

The Sound of Evil

What mournful sound does evil make,
what mantra is its plea?
Are baffling cries we hear opaque,
what mournful sound does evil make?
Is it the cries of a child's heartache
when it was slaughtered at Wounded Knee?
What mournful sound does evil make,
what mantra is its plea?

Lakota Sioux Dream Catcher

Beware The Rattlesnake

Native American Pow Wow

Sad Chapter In History

They lived their lives on sacred ground,
surrendered blood to a trail of tears.
Herded like sheep to army compounds,
they lived their lives on sacred ground.
Cherokee tribes Oklahoma bound,
thousands died in want and fear.
They lived their lives on sacred ground,
surrendered blood to a trail of tears.

Children

Our children are at best on loan,
in our charge for but a day.
Their agendas remain their own,
our children are at best on loan.
Adolescents set a different tone,
charting paths in their own way.
Our children are at best on loan,
in our charge for but a day.

Cup of Love

When our mold is filled with pain
a cup of love is in the furnace.
A bright new day is our refrain,
when our mold is filled with pain.
All our sorrow is but gain,
if we explore life's truth in earnest.
When our mold is filled with pain
a cup of love is in the furnace.

Copyright

Fear of life brings gloom of night,
covers morning sun with clouds.
Worries cling like parasites,
fear of life brings gloom of night.
New morning sun our copyright,
no room for looming shrouds.
Fear of life brings gloom of night
covers morning sun with clouds.

Caught on Camera

Life, a series of programmed lessons
designed to teach us how to love.
Makes no difference our direction,
life, a series of programmed lessons.
Karma records in detailed perfection,
wide-angle lens views all from above.
Life, a series of programmed lessons
designed to teach us how to love.

Sharing Light

To light a candle for others,
does not diminish my flame.

It unites me with sisters and brothers,
to light a candle for others.

Illuminated minds soon discover,
we are different, yet all are the same.

To light a candle for others,
does not diminish my flame.

Bodie Island Lighthouse

Friends

Friends are mirrors on the wall,
they mimic our reflection.

They give the mind direct recall,
friends are mirrors on the wall.

When we run and when we fall,
they give with no rejection.

Friends are mirrors on the wall,
they mimic our reflection.

Enlightenment

Knowledge acquired by
tongue and pen,
wisdom perceived by soul.
Teachers can tell us where
and when,
knowledge acquired by
tongue and pen.
Halls of learning truly a
friend,
millions of facts there are
told.
Knowledge acquired by tongue and pen,
wisdom perceived by soul.

Turkey Vulture

It's Elementary

This world is elementary school,
diplomas clutched in Satan's hand.
No rite negates Creator's rule,
this world is elementary school.
Black prints on white, the world is dual,
"learn how to love," the base command.
This world is elementary school,
diplomas clutched in Satan's hand.

Hummingbird's Song

Hummingbird humming throughout the day,
sips sugar dew from a bottle.
Drinking sweet nectar and darting away,
hummingbird humming throughout the day.
Primrose is sad but it has no say,
its tears produce only mottle.
Hummingbird humming throughout the day,
sips sugar dew from a bottle.

Fade and Bloom

In autumn flowers fade away,
in spring return to bloom again.
Bright colors appear but never stay,
in autumn flowers fade away.
The Creator's signature written in clay,
life finds its peak then fade begins.
In autumn flowers fade away,
in spring return to bloom again.

Male and Female

Two parts, one principle dwells inside,
together in harmony they become one.

Male and female stand with pride,
two parts, one principle dwells inside.

Opposing templates in hearts reside,
harmonic balance can't be outdone.

Two parts, one principle dwells inside,
together in harmony they become one.

Neutral Force

When fear and darkness turn to light
no beastly shadows can be found.

Illusion's mystery will take flight,
when fear and darkness turn to light.

Creative thoughts dance with delight,
adverse forces on neutral ground.

When fear and darkness turn to light
no beastly shadows can be found.

Cattleya Orchid

Knowing

I know that I exist,
I did not create myself.
On this I must insist,
I know that I exist.
My need to know persists,
no other option left,
I know that I exist,
I did not create myself.

Flower Talk

My mother talked as she watered,
the flowers responded with bloom.
A lesson to both sons and daughters,
my mother talked as she watered.
No textbook could ever have taught her
that flowers desired to commune.
My mother talked as she watered,
the flowers responded with bloom.

Forever Now

The eternal now is
here to stay,
reflects each thought
and action.
Time suspends
beyond the fray,
the eternal now is
here to stay.
Viewpoints align in
personal ways,
conceived by unique
attractions.
The eternal now is here to stay,
reflects each thought and action.

*Mt. McKinley
3:15 a.m*

Furt Seal

Fur Seal

He barks to protect his cow,
a warning to keep me at bay.
I want a photo, but how,
he barks to protect his cow.
The time for exposure is now,
I hide behind rocks on the way.
He barks to protect his cow,
a warning to keep me at bay.

Journey to Forever

When this life has come and gone
another woman shall bear me.
Heaven or hell sounds so wrong,
when this life has come and gone.
When I can sing creation's song,
then in my soul I will be free.
When this life has come and gone
another woman shall bear me.

Robin Eggs

Robin feeding young

Awareness Rising

In search of freedom's pleasure,
desire, the shackle that binds.
Want grips life in full measure,
in search of freedom's pleasure.
Awareness exposes a treasure,
leaves worn-out baggage behind.
In search of freedom's pleasure,
desire, the shackle that binds.

Gulls

Good and Evil

Evil, uncontrolled desire,
good in search of meaning.
Moral principles we admire,
evil, uncontrolled desire.
Wicked wears a grim attire,
transforms to good with cleaning.
Evil, uncontrolled desire,
good in search of meaning.

Writing Spiders

Turn Signals

In autumn leaves turn yellow-red
to signal frost is on the way.
Bulbs and blooms are put to bed,
in autumn leaves turn yellow-red.
The law of nature has clearly said,
full glory will return by May.
In autumn leaves turn yellow-red
to signal frost is on the way.

Music of the Spheres

Creation speaks with soft, silent sound,
each note a singing sensation.
In the quark of each atom music is found,
creation speaks with soft, silent sound.
In planets and strings vibrations abound,
in respect to orientation.
Creation speaks with soft, silent sound,
each note a singing sensation.

Flowers and Weeds

What be the difference of flowers and
weeds,
if not for concepts planted in the mind?

Sunshine and rain supplies both their
needs,
what be the difference of flowers and
weeds?

Each born in spring from tiny brown
seeds,
hard crusty hulls soon left far behind.

What be the difference of flowers and
weeds,
if not for concepts planted in the mind?

Black-eyed Susan

Light and sound

Structure of life designed by sound,
revealed to the eye by light.

No matter if square, ragged or round,
structure of life designed by sound.

Unified rhythms of strings abound,
melody reveals copyright.

Structure of life, designed by sound,
revealed to the eye by light.

Life's Diversity

The units of life total one,
expressed in endless reflections.
Like light rays beamed from the sun,
the units of life total one.
The creative process is done,
available for open inspection.
The units of life total one,
expressed in endless reflections.

*Shaggy-stalked Bolete
Mushroom*

Power of Love

The power of love is free to all,
returns in kind for sharing.
Suffused beyond the tallest wall,
the power of love is free to all.
No threatening fears or quick
recall,
unquenchable and caring.
The power of love is free to all,
returns in kind for sharing.

Laughter

Sound of laughter tunes fabric of soul
like a bow on violin strings.
Each note vibrates in sync with the whole,
sound of laughter tunes fabric of soul.
Reverberant music adds notes to the scroll,
fills the heart with joy as it sings.
Sound of laughter tunes fabric of soul
like a bow on violin strings.

Life in the Berry Patch

Every berry has its briar
to prick my hand with pain.
I love to taste fruits of desire,
every berry has its briar.
To harvest what I most admire,
love and honor must remain.
Every berry has its briar
to prick my hand with pain.

Winter Delight

The evergreens stand tall and white,
along a rushing mountain stream.
Turns winter's drab to pure delight,
the evergreens stand tall and white.
Springtime blooms a distant sight,
lush green meadows a fading dream.
The evergreens stand tall and white,
above a rushing mountain stream.

One In Clay

All in life that exists today
in reality has always been.
Precisely formed in Creator's clay,
all in life that exists today.
Life eternally works this way,
DNA designed from within.
All in life that exist today
in reality has always been.

No Greater Love

Our food is a gift from
another,
one life surrenders, one
life survives.
Life gives to life like a
brother,
our food is a gift from
another.
When sharing our food
we discover
we're eating what once
was alive.
Our food is a gift from
another,
one life surrenders, one life survives.

A Fairy's Picnic Table

Anhinga with Fish Dinner

Truth and Love

Truth a song in an open
mind,
love sings to an open heart.
Bonded as one they
vibrate in kind,
truth a song in an open
mind.
A tuning fork most
perfectly timed,
harmony fills every part.
Truth a song in an open
mind,
love sings to an open heart.

Our Home

Our home is shelter from the storm,
true love abides within.
Four walls do not a lovebond form,
our home is shelter from the storm.
A quiet talk, a fireplace warm,
with ones we love and lifelong friends.
Our home is shelter from the storm,
true love abides within.

Seasons of the Heart

Pain, a season of the heart,
like winter breaks our comfort shell.
Required adventure harshly tart,
pain a season of the heart.
Offers soul a virgin start,
slows the spinning carousel.
Pain a season of the heart,
like winter, breaks the comfort shell.

Physical Love

Feather soft skin makes temperature rise,
lips touching lips causes fever.
You in my arms a sensual prize,
feather soft skin makes temperature rise.
Hunger for love could be lust in disguise,
passion on the fly a convivial deceiver.
Feather soft skin makes temperature rise,
lips touching lips causes fever.

Common Murre

Emotional Love

Your vision a river that flooded my heart
when first my eyes fell soft upon you.
No power on earth could make me depart,
your vision a river that flooded my heart.
Fantasy leaped tall mountains to start,
winning your favor in constant review.
Your vision a river that flooded my heart
when first my eyes fell soft upon you.

Mushrooms with young

Time-Track Love

Try to remember when our love was young,
starlight and fireflies danced in the night.
Harmonic musing brought music to tongue,
try to remember when our love was young.
From fruits of affection a ripe vintage sprung,
no room for pretending or false appetite.
Try to remember when our love was young,
starlight and fireflies danced in the night.

Chorus Frogs with Eggs

Mental Love

Very often I know what you're thinking
before words ever pass through your lips.
This connection took years in its making,
very often I know what you're thinking.
A product of mental reshaping,
constantly nursing the script.
Very often I know what you're thinking
before words ever pass through your lips.

Snowy Owls

Spiritual Love

Two souls, one spirit, walk the
beach hand-in-hand,
twin auras united in love's
harmony.
Old sun-wrinkled feet
splashing ocean's wet sand,
two souls, one spirit, walk the
beach hand-in-hand.
Love's freedom in action, no
awkward demand,
peace flowing like music in soft
symphony.
Two souls one spirit, walk the
beach hand in hand,
twin auras united in love's
harmony.

Passion with Reason

Passion adorned with reason
makes life a joyous song.
Music for every season,
passion adorned with reason.
Soul's exaltation is pleasin'
life's natural beauty made strong.
Passion adorned with reason
makes life a joyous song.

Passion Flower

Pictures in the Mind

Images planted in the mind
affect our thoughts and actions.
They light our way or make us blind,
images planted in the mind.
To find ourselves we redesign,
create our own attractions.
Images planted in the mind
affect our thoughts and actions.

Measuring Time

What is time that man should measure,
what magic potion does it hold?
Is it dispensed with daunting pleasure,
what is time that man should measure?
Does it hold majestic treasure,
gates of jasper, streets of gold?
What is time that man should measure,
what magic potion does it hold?

Long Ride to Nowhere

The sound of your voice is my pain,
as I cringe in my prison hell.
The flashback of memories my chain,
the sound of your voice is my pain.
The sorrows I caused you remain,
I withered from evil's dark spell.
The sound of your voice is my pain,
as I cringe in my prison hell.

Life in the Pilloy

Riding the Wheel

What goes around can come again
as history has recorded.
A golden halo yields to sin,
what goes around can come again.
A wooden cross with swastika bends,
the German church contorted.
What goes around can come again
as history has recorded.

Wheel of Life

The scheme of life allows no waste,
discarded loss is born anew.
Life's essence moves at its own pace,
the scheme of life allows no waste.
Life's gift to life, its saving grace,
death gives fungus quick debut.
The scheme of life allows no waste,
discarded loss is born anew.

Chanterelle
Mushroom

Marmot

Reality

Science calls it evolution,
religion, creative design.

What is the right resolution?
Science calls it evolution.

Reality allows no dilution,
it rises beyond space and time.

Science calls it evolution,
religion, creative design.

Rhyme Time

The ebb and flow of rhythmic rhyme,
italic words to remember.

They resonate in every line,
the ebb and flow of rhythmic rhyme.

Harmonic words transcending time
ignite life's glowing embers.

The ebb and flow of rhythmic rhyme,
italic words to remember.

Northern Mocking Bird

True Love

True love will flow
forever,
like waves between two
shores.
No force can ever sever,
true love will flow forever.
Its power a grand
endeavor,
the sea its metaphor.
True love will flow
forever,
like waves between two
shores.

Beyond Human Hands

What man can alter speed of light,
or command reverse to gait of sound.
Light flies unseen to human sight,
what man can alter speed of light.
The Creator owns every copyright,
man's feeble hands are bound.
What man can alter speed of light,
or command reverse to gait of sound.

Footprints

Footprints planted in salty sand
chart detailed maps of where I've been.
They count the same on sea or land,
footprints planted in salty sand.
If measured by foot or by the hand,
they steer life's course from deep within.
Footprints planted in salty sand
chart detailed maps of where I've been.

Equinox of Life

When hair turns silver and wrinkles unfold
the autumn of life brings reflection.
Stories of youth are told and retold,
when hair turns silver and wrinkles unfold.
Lessons of life are stenciled in bold,
giving soul a sense of direction.
When hair turns silver and wrinkles unfold
the autumn of life brings reflection .

The Comma

Butterfly is Born

Death, a comma in the book of life,
refreshing new beginning.
Short recess from a world of strife,
death, a comma in the book of life.
If by disease or by the knife,
awareness soul is winning.
Death, a comma in the book of life,
refreshing new beginning.